DEDICATED TO MY AMAZING PUBLISHER DARLENE WHO HAS BEEN WITH ME EVERY STEP OF THE WAY. WITHOUT YOU, THIS WOULD NEVER HAVE BEEN POSSIBLE. TO MY WONDERFUL HUSBAND, GRANT, YOUR SUPPORT, FAITH, AND BELIEF IN ME MEANS MORE THAN YOU WILL EVER KNOW.

THE LONELY HEDGEHOG

S.J.LONGSTAFF

ILLUSTRATIONS BY MADISON HOCKER

Hector hedgehog loves to play,

but there is something standing in his way.

He's new in town,
and has no friends,
but this isn't where
the story ends.

One morning Hector goes for a walk in the park,

As he passes a group of squirrels, he hears a hurtful remark...

He starts to walk fast,
to make his way **home**,

He has never felt
so sad and **alone**.

When he passes a pack of rats,

Hector begins to run faster and faster,
His morning walk turns into a disaster.

He runs past a badger
who gives him
an awkward stare,
He closes his eyes to avoid the glare.

Hector runs rapid and trips
with a thud, and all of a sudden…,

He lands straight in the

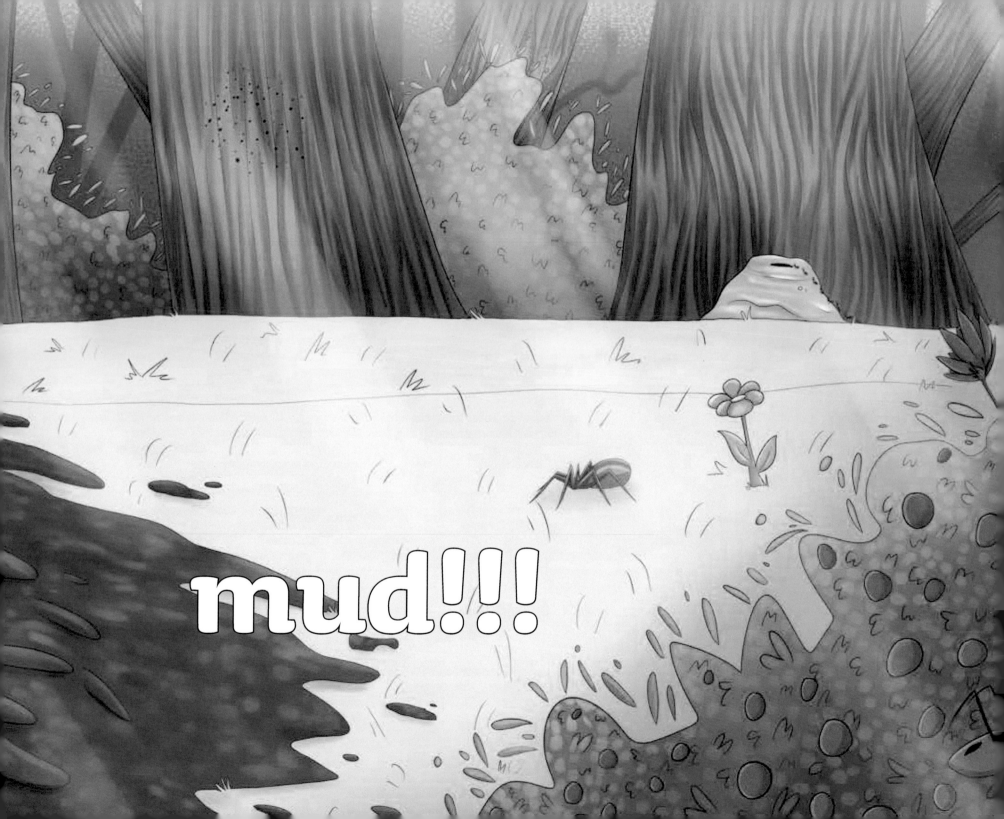

He curls into a ball
as everyone laughs,
He knows he has to
get back on the path.

To make his way home,
where he is safe and **sound**,
Just then, he hears a noise
so he looks **around**.

A soft, gentle voice says,
"Are you ok? Here take my hand."
Hector looks up, he doesn't understand.

Before him stands a big fluffy rabbit,
She holds out her paw so Hector can grab it.

She smiles, "Not everyone is mean.
Just you wait, and you'll see…"
Hector's face lights up with glee.

Hector says, "Hello"
to all the friendly faces,

And he knows he
moved to the best
of places.

The Lonely Hedgehog was born from the heart of a mother who wanted to bring memorable life lessons to her children. S.J. Longstaff lives in the UK with her three adorable children and the love of her life, Grant. She loves writing and all things Christmas. This is Longstaff's first book.

Ingram Content Group UK Ltd.
Milton Keynes UK
UKRC030958140323
418554UK00001B/6